To Joel, Morgan and Flynn (the demolition boy)
and also to Celia and James,
with massive thanks for everything — A.M.

Can you spot
the crab
throughout
the book?

EGMONT
We bring stories to life

First published in Great Britain 2015 by Egmont UK Limited
This edition published 2018 by Dean,
an imprint of Egmont UK Limited,
The Yellow Building, 1 Nicholas Road, London, W11 4AN
www.egmont.co.uk

Text and illustrations copyright © Angie Morgan 2015
Angie Morgan has asserted her moral rights.
All photographs courtesy of Shutterstock.

ISBN 978 0 603 57567 9

70167/001

Printed in Malaysia

A CIP catalogue record for this title is available
from the British Library.

Egmont takes its responsibility to the planet and its inhabitants very seriously.
All the papers we use are from well-managed forests run by responsible suppliers.

SHOUTY ARTHUR
at the Seaside

Angie Morgan

Arthur and Edith were going to the seaside.

Arthur was VERY excited.

"Will I like it at the seaside, Edith?" asked Arthur.

"Yes, it's completely BRILLIANT," said Edith. "There's ...

...ice creams

...and sandcastles

...and seagulls

...and shells

. . .and rockpools."

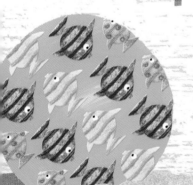

"But you have to remember not to be shouty," said Edith.
"People don't like it if you're too shouty."

"I know, Edith," shouted Arthur.

"I promise I'll be my VERY quietest."

RAAA!

Arthur had SUCH a lovely time...

. . . that he forgot
all about not
being shouty.

"Let's build a sandcastle," said Edith.

"YAY!"

shouted Arthur.

So Edith built a sandcastle
and Arthur dug a moat all around it.

"GO, YOU OLD SANDCASTLE!"

Arthur had SUCH a lovely time...

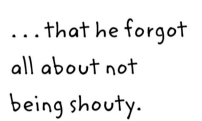

. . . that he forgot
all about not
being shouty.

"We could play pirates in this
boat, Arthur," said Edith.

Arthur loved playing pirates.

"YO-HO-HO!"

shouted Pirate Arthur.

"GO, YOU OLD PIRATES!"

"ARRR!"

Arthur had SUCH a lovely time...

. . . that he forgot all about not being shouty.

"I'm a little bit fed up, Edith," said Arthur. "You said the seaside was brilliant, but it's not!"

"That's because you're being too shouty,"
said Edith. "Let's go and get some ice cream."

So Arthur and Edith ate their ice creams
and all the people on the beach enjoyed
the peace and quiet.

When they had finished their ice creams,
Arthur asked, "What shall I do now, Edith?"

Edith thought for a moment. "Why don't you see
how fast you can run to those rocks and back?"

So Arthur ran as fast as he could all the way to the rocks.

When Arthur didn't come back, Edith went to look for him.

"LOOK, EDITH," shouted Arthur. "A ROCKPOOL!"

"Wow!" said Edith.

Arthur and Edith looked at the rockpool for ages and ages.

Then Edith said it was time to go.

"There's an awful lot of sea," said Arthur.
"I'm sure there wasn't that much a little while ago."

"Oh dear," said Edith. "Arthur, could you be really shouty now, please?"

So Arthur shouted his very loudest.

And Edith shouted too!

"HEEEELP!"

When the rescue boat came, Arthur was so excited he thought he would burst.

RESCUE

"You were right, Edith," said Arthur.
"The seaside is completely BRILLIANT...

...but you were wrong about being shouty. Sometimes it can be REALLY useful!"

Arthur's Guide to ROCKPOOLS
and what's IN them.

There are...

CRABS
(hermit)

STARFISH

FISH (small ones mostly)

SHRIMP

MUSSELS

SEA ANEMONES

SEAWEED

BARNACLES
(these are asleep)